# SNAPPSY
## THE ALLIGATOR

AND HIS BEST FRIEND FOREVER!

Probably

Words by Julie Falatko • Pictures by Tim Miller

VIKING

Snappsy the alligator was the most interesting reptile in the whole world.

He was taller than the tallest tree.

He delighted crowds at the jamboree.

And once he jumped over 23 cars on his scooter.

He's my very best friend.

We met at a party. And now we do everything together.

Snappsy the alligator led his very best friend in a conga line all the way to…

LIBRARY
I have to stop at the library to return these books.
BONK!
BONK!
BONK!

Snappsy the alligator, who only occasionally stayed at home by himself, set off to plan for a night of fun with his very best friend.

And Snappsy the alligator and his BFF had a lovely evening doing the things that best friends do.

They had such a wonderful time that they decided Bert should move in.

*For Carter and Elizabeth,*
*the sparkliest BFFs a writer could ever want.*
—J.F.


*To Susan,*
*art teacher extraordinaire and champion of the arts like no other.*
—T.M.

VIKING
Penguin Young Readers Group
An imprint of Penguin Random House LLC
375 Hudson Street
New York, New York 10014

First published in the United States of America by Viking,
an imprint of Penguin Random House LLC, 2017

Text copyright © 2017 by Julie Falatko
Illustrations copyright © 2017 by Tim Miller

LIBRARY OF CONGRESS CATALOGING-IN-PUBLICATION DATA IS AVAILABLE
ISBN: 9780425288658

Set in ITC Cheltenham and ITC American Typewriter
Printed in China

1  3  5  7  9  10  8  6  4  2

The pictures in this book were made with brush and ink and
computer hocus-pocus.

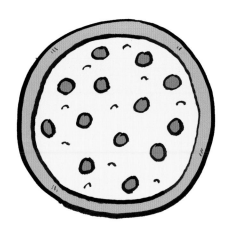